Little Red

Bethan Woollvin

PEACHTREE
ATLANTA

Chris, Jim, and my

whole family,

I couldn't have done

it without you.

—B. W.

Published by
Peachtree Publishers
1700 Chattahoochee Avenue
Atlanta, Georgia 30318-2112
www.peachtree-online.com

Text and illustrations © 2016 by Bethan Woollvin

First published in Great Britain in 2016 by Two Hoots, an imprint of Pan Macmillan
First United States version published in 2016 by Peachtree Publishers

Illustrations created in gouache and digital

Printed in November 2016 in China
10 9 8 7 6 5 4 3 2

ISBN 978-1-56145-917-9

Library of Congress Cataloging-in-Publication Data

Names: Woollvin, Bethan.
Title: Little Red / by Bethan Woollvin.
Description: Atlanta, GA : Peachtree Publishers, [2016] | Summary: "On her way to Grandma's house,
Little Red meets a wolf. Which might scare some little girls. But not this little girl. She knows just what
the wolf is up to, and she's not going to let him get away with it"—Provided by publisher.
Identifiers: LCCN 2015034204
Subjects: | CYAC: Fairy tales. | Folklore.
Classification: LCC PZ8.W913 Li 2016 | DDC 398.2—dc23
LC record available at http://lccn.loc.gov/2015034204

One day, Little Red's mother called to her.

"Please take some cake to your Grandma," she said.
"She's not feeling too well."

So Little Red set off on her
journey through the forest
to Grandma's house.

Before long, she met a wolf.

"Where are you going?" he growled.

Which might have scared some little girls.

But not this little girl.

"To my Grandma's," Little Red replied.

"She's not feeling well."

"Is that right?" asked the wolf.

And he made a plan.

The wolf said good-bye to
Little Red, took a shortcut through
the trees, and found Grandma's house.

Which was unlucky for Grandma.

He put on her glasses and spare nightdress,
and climbed into her bed.

And there he waited.

It wasn't long before Little Red arrived
and found that the door to Grandma's
house was already open. She peeped in
through the window.

She couldn't see Grandma,
but she could see a badly disguised
wolf waiting in Grandma's bed!

Which might have scared
some little girls.
But not this little girl.

She made a plan
and went inside.

"Hello, Grandma," Little Red said,
though she wasn't fooled for a minute.

"Oh, Grandma! What big ears
you have!" she said.

"Oh, Grandma! What big eyes
you have!" she said.

And, "Oh, Grandma! What *big* teeth you have!" she said.

"Why yes, my dear," replied the wolf.
"All the better to..."

"EAT YOU WITH!"

And the wolf leaped forward.

Which might have scared
some little girls...

...but not this little girl.

Which was unlucky for the wolf.